The Tangled Skirt

by Steve Braunstein

A SAMUEL FRENCH ACTING EDITION

SAMUEL FRENCH

FOUNDED 1830

SAMUELFRENCH.COM

Samuel French, Inc.
45 West 25th Street
New York, NY 10010

www.SamuelFrench.com

FOR PRODUCTION INQUIRIES
Info@SamuelFrench.com
1-866-598-8449

THE TANGLED SKIRT was first produced by the New Jersey Repertory Company in Long Branch, New Jersey on December 4, 2010. The performance was directed by Evan Bergman, with sets by Jessica Parks, costumes by Patricia E. Doherty, sound by Nathan Leigh, and lighting by Jill Nagle. The Production Stage Manager was Rose Riccardi. The cast was as follows:

BAILEY . . . . Vince Nappo

RHONDA. . . . . Carmit Levité

I would like to gratefully acknowledge Artistic Director SuzAnne Barabas and Executive Producer Gabor Barabas for giving this play such an outstanding, first-rate debut.

-*S.B.*

CHARACTERS

BAILEY BRYCE – Enigmatic, small town denizen; mid 30s-early 40s.

RHONDA CLAIRE – A stranger in town, to die for; in her 30s.

SETTING

A Small Town Bus Depot

TIME

At The Start Of The Play, 12:30 am

AUTHOR'S NOTES

The play occurs in real time with no intermission.

Did you ever pass through a small town and feel as though you've just gone back in time? Maybe it's economic conditions, or quaint, old fashioned values, or just neglect. Either way, this place just feels locked in another era. Such is the bus station setting of *THE TANGLED SKIRT*. It might be today, but this location starkly evokes many decades past to be sure. The play walks a stylistic tightrope; a modern day tale of greed, need and deadly deeds that gives a nuanced nod to the smoky noirs of the 40s and 50s. People have asked me if I suggest watching some classic noir-styled movies as they prepare to do the play. Sure. Watch them and savor them. Take in the snap and slap of the storytelling and performances. Study the feel and flow, but don't pick up too much. I don't specify year and locality in my directions to enhance the timelessness of the themes. This is a contemporary thriller about the dangers of unharnessed and misguided desires – for people and things. Whether we want to think it or not, Bailey Bryce and Rhonda Claire, the characters in this story, are not so different from you or me. Except, maybe their desperation pushes them farther. Anyway, the dreams and schemes that drive them are universal; sometimes the things we crave most are just out of reach. Tough. Tragic. And true. It was then, it is now, and always will be…no matter where – or when – the bus of life drops you off.

For Ruthi
who liked a good twist

(A dimly lit bus depot in the middle of nowhere. The place is deserted. The whole station is just a few benches and a closed snack counter. Maybe a payphone, a newspaper machine. A chalk board reads:

LAST BUS. THUNDER BAY. 2:00 am.)

(The depot clock reads 12:30 am. Dark. Desolate. Uninviting. There seems no reason in the world any living soul would be in this grim place, especially at this ungodly hour. But there is a living soul about to arrive. And there is a reason.)

(Enter **BAILEY BRYCE**, *dapperly dressed, holding a duffle bag, and breathless from running. He scans the depot, relieved, for the moment, that he is alone.* **BAILEY** *takes a few, shaky deep breaths. He grips his bag tightly, noting the clock and the Thunder Bay bus time. He is clearly on edge, but is determined to keep it all together. He nervously glances out the smudgy depot window, and scans again the shadowy dive. He sits down and pulls from his bag a small voice recorder. He thinks a moment, then switches it on.)*

BAILEY. There was no moon on this dark, dank night. The rain slick streets a relentless reminder that this is indeed a slippery world. The faint light inside the teetering bus depot offered little illumination, emitting, instead, the fatal glimmer of dread. He sat alone in the deserted station, his isolation looming as its own unnerving threat. A prelude, a warning perhaps, of what this moonless night had in store for him. He wondered, if he vanished that night, never to be seen or heard from again, if anyone would know. If anyone would care. He knew the terrible answer, but was more concerned about getting a proper burial.

Everyone should get a proper burial. Even people like him. But he knew, more likely, some overly curious kids, poking around where they shouldn't be poking, will find his bones, fifty years from now, brittle and nameless in the dirt. They'll be too dumb to know at that tender age that things you touch, especially things you shouldn't, become part of you forever.

(**BAILEY** *gets up and moves again to the smudged window, gazing out.*)

BAILEY. The images of prying kids faded from his thoughts. Eclipsed by reveries of a moonless sky, a bus to Thunder Bay...

(*He sits.*)

And the elusive nature of fate.

(**RHONDA**, *a looker to boot, enters the depot.* **BAILEY** *turns and watches her. He speaks softly into the recorder.*)

Then...she walked in.

(**BAILEY** *observes* **RHONDA**, *who is not yet aware of him. She is decked out to the nines, way, way out of place in this mucky locus. She seems rushed, breathless. She anxiously checks the bus schedule and the clock. She is flustered, gripping tight her travel bag. Alarmed, she smoothes her tousled, designer skirt.*)

BAILEY. *(cont.) (into recorder)* She was a sight for his weary, jaded eyes. The kind of woman you'd thank for tearing your heart out just because she took the trouble to look at you. You could tell by the way she stood there, the way she carried herself, the way she did nothing, that she's ruined lots of men in her time. He thought about where *her* bones might end up.

(**RHONDA** *glances around for a seat. She now notices* **BAILEY**, *who's placed the recorder back into his bag. She finds a seat away from* **BAILEY**, *and brushes it with her hand. The dirt is too much. Disgusted and agitated, she approaches* **BAILEY**'s *bench. She gazes at it, and at him.*)

RHONDA. You mind?

BAILEY. All yours.

(**RHONDA** *sits on the far end of the bench.*)

RHONDA. Place gives me the shivers.

BAILEY. Not much light, that's for sure.

RHONDA. No place for a woman.

BAILEY. That's for sure, too.

RHONDA. Lots of creeps out there. Lots of hands. Place like this…drifters and loners. This hour. No security. Like people who take the bus have no virtue.

BAILEY. Do we?

RHONDA. What?

BAILEY. I'm Bailey. Bailey Bryce.

RHONDA. Oh. Rhonda. Rhonda Claire. From Thunder Bay.

BAILEY. Going home?

RHONDA. Yeah. It's been a while. You from there, too?

BAILEY. No. I'm from here. But I've got business there.

RHONDA. What do you do, Bailey?

BAILEY. How do you know I'm not a loner drifter creep?

RHONDA. A loner drifter creep named Bailey Bryce? I doubt that.

BAILEY. I've got hands.

RHONDA. I study the backs of heads. I can tell a person's character just by looking.

BAILEY. That's a gift. To be able to do that.

RHONDA. You've got a gift, Bailey?

BAILEY. I tell stories.

RHONDA. What's that mean?

BAILEY. I'm a storyteller.

RHONDA. To who?

BAILEY. To anyone who will listen.

RHONDA. Is that your business in Thunder Bay? To tell stories?

BAILEY. If they'll listen.

RHONDA. That's how you live? Telling stories?

BAILEY. How do you live, Rhonda Claire?

RHONDA. Me? I...married well.

BAILEY. I don't see a ring.

RHONDA. You're very observant.

BAILEY. Storytellers are observers of sorts.

RHONDA. You tell true stories, Bailey?

BAILEY. All stories are true. Every one.

RHONDA. I never thought of that. Yeah. For someone out there I guess anything you can imagine has happened.

BAILEY. That's why they work.

RHONDA. Well, you're the first person I've ever met who called himself a storyteller. I guess it's a small town thing.

BAILEY. Thunder Bay so big?

RHONDA. Anywhere's bigger than here.

BAILEY. *(smiles)* Yeah. Lots of maps don't have us. Just a spot on the world.

RHONDA. Maybe if they had more buses...

BAILEY. Sure. And more light. Yeah. No postcards of this place.

(They laugh softly.)

No one ever comes here. What reason could there possibly be? On the other hand, I find it quaint.

RHONDA. To each his own.

(They go silent a moment.)

BAILEY. When did he die?

RHONDA. Who?

BAILEY. Your husband.

RHONDA. My...? Well, where on Earth did you...did you come up with such a ridiculous –

BAILEY. Am I right?

*(**RHONDA** gets up shakily.)*

RHONDA. My life is *my* business.

BAILEY. Sometimes I'm too observant for my own good.

RHONDA. *(muttering)* Don't talk to strangers. First thing you learn.

(**RHONDA** *fidgets by the dim snack counter.*)

Make you wait so long for a bus. Think they'd offer coffee. Gum. Something.

BAILEY. Yeah. I guess it's like you said. We've got no virtue.

(**BAILEY** *fishes through his pockets.*)

Usually carry a lozenge.

RHONDA. Don't bother. But thanks.

(a siren in the distance)

BAILEY. They're like candy.

(**RHONDA** *looks out the window.* **BAILEY** *has patted every pocket.*)

Oh, well. In my other suit, I guess. I have another suit.

RHONDA. I don't really want anything. I just...you know. It's the waiting.

(**RHONDA** *paces; tense, shaky.* **BAILEY** *watches her.*)

BAILEY. Anticipation. In the station. Waiting for a bus. It will arrive. You will likely survive. So what is all the fuss?

(**RHONDA** *looks at him, unamused.*)

RHONDA. You just make that up?

BAILEY. You inspired me. Impressed?

RHONDA. *(not really)* Sure, Bailey.

BAILEY. That's not to say I'm good at everything. That would be overkill. But I do have a way of putting people at ease. I have that kind of personality. People just like me.

RHONDA. I'm happy for you.

BAILEY. You like me, Rhonda Claire?

RHONDA. I...don't know you.

BAILEY. Well, not intimately. But you're getting the gist.

RHONDA. *(agitated)* What's the difference? We're just waiting for a bus together. Look, I don't mean to be rude, but I'd rather not…you know, get into some personal thing with you.

BAILEY. You mean like your husband.

RHONDA. *(flustered)* For example, yes. Let's just talk about the weather or not talk at all.

(**RHONDA** *stands off to the side, collecting herself.* **BAILEY** *is quiet for a moment.*)

BAILEY. Rained earlier.

RHONDA. Yes. I know.

BAILEY. I'm glad we get the seasons here. I like the changes. I like when the leaves turn. But I like the sheen of the frozen lake in the winter, too.

(**RHONDA** *is silent, preoccupied.*)

What's it like in Thunder Bay?

(**RHONDA** *recoils.*)

That's not personal.

RHONDA. It's where I'm from.

BAILEY. It's a climate question.

(**RHONDA** *sits on the far end of the bench*)

RHONDA. When it's cold, it's cold.

BAILEY. Really.

RHONDA. I hope you packed warm. If you intend to stay.

BAILEY. I'd never leave this place forever.

RHONDA. Yes. You fit here.

BAILEY. It's all I know of the world. Everything I need is here.

RHONDA. Then why are you leaving?

BAILEY. I'm not leaving. I'm just going away.

RHONDA. I won't be a hypocrite and pry.

BAILEY. I'll tell you anything.

RHONDA. I don't need to know your story.

BAILEY. It's free.

RHONDA. Knowing people always comes with a price. And you don't look cheap.

BAILEY. You've been burned.

RHONDA. Set on fire. But there you go again.

BAILEY. It wasn't a question. It was an –

RHONDA. Stop observing me, Bailey.

BAILEY. But…you're right here. Where else do I look?

RHONDA. I don't mean to be impolite. But it's just a little unnerving being alone in this dark heap so late at night.

BAILEY. You're…um…not alone.

RHONDA. You know what I mean.

BAILEY. You said you weren't afraid of me.

RHONDA. That's before you talked.

BAILEY. What did I say?

RHONDA. Forget it. Please.

BAILEY. Oh. The husband.

RHONDA. It rained earlier.

BAILEY. I'm just nobody. Don't worry.

RHONDA. I don't scare easy. It's just…I'm away from home.

BAILEY. And it's dark.

RHONDA. And it's dark.

(They go silent a moment.)

BAILEY. Gets dark in Thunder Bay I imagine.

RHONDA. Well sure.

(BAILEY stands up)

BAILEY. How dark?

(RHONDA tries to contain her agitation)

RHONDA. What an odd question.

BAILEY. They got a moon there?

RHONDA. The whole world's got a moon.

BAILEY. Not here.

RHONDA. Well, not tonight. Sometimes it's just not there.

BAILEY. *(amused)* Where could it be? Who's got the moon? You got it, Rhonda Claire?

RHONDA. Sure. Right there in my bag. With the stars, the solar system and my stockings.

BAILEY. I once promised a girl the moon.

RHONDA. What she get instead?

(**BAILEY** *sighs, leaning against the snack counter.*)

BAILEY. Stories.

RHONDA. That's sweet, Bailey.

BAILEY. Yeah. But you can't take stories to the bank.

RHONDA. Oh. She's not your girl now, I take it.

BAILEY. This was, God, so long ago.

RHONDA. You sound…not quite over it.

BAILEY. I'm over her. It was just a hard lesson.

RHONDA. What's the lesson?

BAILEY. Women love money.

RHONDA. Boy.

BAILEY. See. I don't mind opening my soul to a stranger.

RHONDA. I did get sucked in.

BAILEY. It's social intercourse.

RHONDA. I don't need to know more.

BAILEY. But am I wrong?

RHONDA. About what?

BAILEY. About women and money?

RHONDA. Bailey. We're waiting for a bus

BAILEY. We already did the weather.

(**RHONDA** *fidgets, disquieted.*)

RHONDA. I can't speak for all women –

BAILEY. Then you.

RHONDA. What could it possibly matter? We're not dating. We're just killing time in Hell.

(*RHONDA gets up and goes to the window.*)

RHONDA. *(cont.)* Maybe it'll get in early.

BAILEY. I doubt that.

RHONDA. Just let me think it. Okay?

(*RHONDA shakes him off and sits quietly. **BAILEY** sits, too, keeping his distance. Another siren is heard deep in the distance. **BAILEY** perks up a little, but **RHONDA** is oblivious, lost in thought. All is silent again. Until …*)

(softly) What would life be without it?

(***BAILEY** looks at her.*)

Money.

BAILEY. Yeah. Sure.

RHONDA. Don't blame women. It's everybody.

BAILEY. It is everybody. I was too young back then. I didn't know the world outside this town.

RHONDA. You know the world now, Bailey?

BAILEY. I know buses never come early. What else is there?

*(Despite herself, **RHONDA** smiles.)*

Don't take this personally. But I like your smile.

RHONDA. Bailey. Don't. Please.

BAILEY. Don't what?

RHONDA. Don't be a man.

BAILEY. Just because I'm a man doesn't mean I'm after something.

(***RHONDA** looks away, shaking her head.*)

Doesn't mean I'll burn you.

RHONDA. Bailey –

BAILEY. I don't even carry matches.

RHONDA. You can't help it. None of you can.

BAILEY. I'm not going to marry until I'm really in love. That's the mistake people make. They marry for the wrong reasons.

RHONDA. Is that a shot at me?

BAILEY. I'm just saying, my time comes, it'll be true love. True love.

RHONDA. I hope your own story ends well, Bailey.

BAILEY. Me, too. And yours.

RHONDA. That bus'll be a start.

BAILEY. Wherever you go, no matter how far, what's done is done. You're still who you are. What you are.

RHONDA. What's that mean?

BAILEY. I'm just saying…wherever you go…it doesn't change a thing.

RHONDA. *(agitated)* I don't want to change a thing. I like just where I am.

BAILEY. This hole?

RHONDA. I don't mean it like that. I mean I like where I am in life. It wasn't always the case.

BAILEY. I got that impression.

RHONDA. Sometimes you get chained to people without realizing it. Before you know it, you're trapped.

BAILEY. Like now. With me.

RHONDA. We're not chained together. And I've got my ticket out. Sometimes it seems there is no out. All that lies ahead is hopelessness.

BAILEY. A woman trapped like that…might do anything to escape. Desperate people might resort to desperate measures.

RHONDA. A woman, in particular, shouldn't be judged.

BAILEY. They're different. Women.

RHONDA. Yes. They are.

BAILEY. Your travel bag there. What's that? Kind of a lipstick red?

*(**RHONDA** impulsively puts her arm on the bag.)*

A man wouldn't carry that.

RHONDA. *(softly)* No.

BAILEY. You can get a lot in there I'll bet.

(**RHONDA** *fidgets.*)

BAILEY. *(cont.)* You seem to handle it just fine.

RHONDA. *(uneasy)* I manage.

BAILEY. You unchained yourself from something terrible in Thunder Bay. You can probably handle anything. Even this town.

RHONDA. Some days you're on top of the world. Other days you're trying to crawl out from under it.

BAILEY. And how was this day? On top? Or under?

*(Dogs bark in the distance. **BAILEY** goes to a window.)*

Some commotion …

RHONDA. The wet streets.

BAILEY. The what?

RHONDA. Maybe a car skidded off the road.

BAILEY. Oh. Right.

(The barking fades off.)

People aren't cautious anymore.

RHONDA. Cautious. Careful. What's going to happen is, I don't know, going to happen.

BAILEY. Well, that's the whole mystery. Of life, I mean. Are we all just headed to some pre-planned end?

RHONDA. Now you're getting into destiny. And it's late, Bailey.

BAILEY. Maybe…maybe *this* is destiny.

RHONDA. This? You mean this place?

BAILEY. And…us. You know, maybe our meeting here was pre-destined. Maybe this was meant to be.

RHONDA. You've got 'small town' written all over you.

BAILEY. *(laughing)* I guess some things just can't be erased.

RHONDA. I don't mean it in a bad way.

BAILEY. *(good-natured)* I've heard worse.

(They laugh softly.)

Anything else written on me?

RHONDA. Oh, it's just an expression. I gave up figuring people out long ago.

BAILEY. Why bother. It never works.

RHONDA. You think you've got someone pegged and wham. They're something else entirely.

BAILEY. Like the girl.

RHONDA. The girl? Oh. *Your* girl.

BAILEY. The best part of a relationship, maybe the only good part, is the first thirty minutes.

RHONDA. *(laughing)* That's a dark view of people.

BAILEY. Well, take us. I mean, this part now, right now, is probably the happiest we'll ever be together.

RHONDA. *(gently)* Bailey, we won't know each other after tonight. We're just two people waiting for a bus.

BAILEY. Thank God for that. If only the bus were less than thirty minutes away. There's too much time for this cordial chance meeting to go bad.

RHONDA. *(amused)* Just keep things light and superficial, we'll be fine.

BAILEY. Yes. I have a habit of probing. Life is a story and that's my business. So I have to force myself to close shop.

RHONDA. It's after midnight. Most people are sleeping.

BAILEY. Oh, I know. They're gone. So deep, they're gone.

RHONDA. I envy them.

BAILEY. Really.

RHONDA. Well, I'm not always a good sleeper.

BAILEY. Good people should sleep deep. Clear conscience.

RHONDA. How many people are good?

BAILEY. I sleep like a rock.

RHONDA. It's nice to meet a man so pure.

BAILEY. But psychopaths sleep well too, I read somewhere.

RHONDA. Yes. No remorse.

BAILEY. Is that it?

RHONDA. People with no remorse have the sleep thing down.

BAILEY. So psychos and saints have the sweetest dreams.

RHONDA. I don't know about their dreams. But they sleep.

BAILEY. Well, you learn something every day. Even in this teetering terminal you learn about life. I'm glad we met.

(He looks at her.)

RHONDA. I guess I have to say 'me too'.

BAILEY. It's just manners.

*(**RHONDA** checks her watch. She and **BAILEY** fall silent a moment.)*

He'll be glad to have you home.

RHONDA. Who…?

BAILEY. I don't know if I'd let my wife travel this late. If I had one.

*(**RHONDA** shifts uncomfortably.)*

Lucky I'm here. If I were a husband, I'd very much appreciate someone watching over my wife when she's alone far from home. Will you tell him about me? Maybe I'll get a cigar out of it.

RHONDA. There is no husband. Not anymore.

BAILEY. Well, it's no business of mine. But where'd he go?

RHONDA. He…died. Three years ago.

BAILEY. Sorry. How?

RHONDA. *(defensively)* It was an accident.

BAILEY. Car?

RHONDA. No.

BAILEY. Airplane?

RHONDA. No.

BAILEY. Bathtub?

RHONDA. Mr. Bryce!

*(**RHONDA** moves away from him. **BAILEY** rises slowly.)*

BAILEY. Stairs?

*(**RHONDA**, shaken, turns sharply to him.)*

BAILEY. *(cont.)* Did he slip?

> (**RHONDA**, *wobbled, is silent.*)

> Was he drunk?

> (**RHONDA**, *speechless, cannot respond.*)

> Was it dark?

> (**RHONDA** *holds back tears.* **BAILEY** *moves closer to her.*)

> Was he pushed?

> (**RHONDA**'s *eyes widen. She grabs her bag.*)

RHONDA. If you'll excuse me I'll wait outside.

> (**RHONDA** *hurriedly moves to the door.*)

BAILEY. I wouldn't go out there, Rhonda Claire.

RHONDA. Why not??

BAILEY. Creeps. Drifters.

RHONDA. I'll take my chances.

BAILEY. Killers.

RHONDA. What are you – ?

BAILEY. Don't you know?

RHONDA. Know what??

> (**BAILEY** *looks at her a moment.*)

BAILEY. There was a murder here. In town. Just tonight.

RHONDA. *(shaken)* What happened?

BAILEY. A man was gunned down. Robbed blind. Maybe a million.

RHONDA. In this little town?

BAILEY. Right here. Where everybody knows everybody and everything about everything. Except the killer's identity.

RHONDA. …I had no idea.

BAILEY. Ask me, it's a stranger. I doubt anyone in this cracker barrel whistle-stop even owns a gun. I've lived here all my life. No one ever got killed this way. Not murdered. Here, just old age kills you. Shootings, stabbings, that's like another planet to us. Now it's happened. It's come here, uninvited. From far away. How'd it get here, Rhonda Claire? Who brought this evil to such an innocent place?

RHONDA. Did you...know him?

BAILEY. Him?

RHONDA. *(softly)* The dead man.

BAILEY. I know everybody.

(Rhonda slowly sits.)

RHONDA. Except me.

BAILEY. You're a long way from Thunder Bay. All that distance from Canada just to visit our little, nearly invisible zone of nothingness.

RHONDA. You don't think that I...?

BAILEY. Look, I'm no authority, but a newcomer pops into town then leaves the night a man is killed. It's suspicious.

RHONDA. Look, I have no idea what's going on out there. Or in here, for that matter.

BAILEY. I didn't mean to suggest...

RHONDA. Just let me be. Please.

(She turns away from him, tense and jittery.)

BAILEY. I didn't mean to upset you.

RHONDA. Well you have.

BAILEY. *(broadly)* A thousand pardons.

RHONDA. Don't make light. After accusing me of murder.

BAILEY. I didn't exactly accuse you. I just thought...maybe there's a story here.

*(**RHONDA** turns to him.)*

RHONDA. Did you follow me?

BAILEY. Follow you? I don't even know who you are.

RHONDA. I felt a shadow on me tonight.

BAILEY. I'm not a shadow, Rhonda Claire.

(She stands, quaking.)

RHONDA. Why do you keep calling me that??

BAILEY. What?

RHONDA. Rhonda Claire. My husband...

BAILEY. Your husband?

RHONDA. Nothing.

BAILEY. You mean...he called you Rhonda Claire too.

RHONDA. *(softly)* Yes.

BAILEY. Did he say your name before he died?

RHONDA. *(numbly)* Yes.

BAILEY. At the foot of the stairs?

RHONDA. You can't prove anything. No one was there.

BAILEY . Well. You were.

*(***RHONDA*** gazes at him, distraught.)*

RHONDA. Don't sit next to me on the bus.

BAILEY. I like the window.

RHONDA. Not that it matters. But it was self-defense.

BAILEY. The fall?

*(***RHONDA*** moves closer to ***BAILEY***.)*

RHONDA. I didn't mean for it to happen. He was drunk. Our marriage was good as done. I was preparing to leave that night. He couldn't accept it was over. He pawed me like an animal at the top of the stairs. I resisted. He slapped me so hard the whole room spun. He hit me again. I thought I was going to die. I flung my arms wildly at him. He lost his balance and toppled down.

BAILEY. Was he dead?

RHONDA. I went to see. I approached him slowly. Cautiously. Gripping the banister tight. I stood over him. His eyes were open. That's when he said it. For the very last time. That's when he said, "Rhonda Claire."

*(***BAILEY*** is riveted.)*

You believe me?

BAILEY. I want to.

RHONDA. When you get to Thunder Bay, check with the police. They took my picture that night.

BAILEY. You were booked.

RHONDA. I was beaten. Look at my face in those pictures. It'll keep you up nights.

BAILEY. Was he rich?

RHONDA. Okay, Bailey. You got me. He was. At least when I married him. But he was a gambler, too. When it became an addiction, he lost everything. Including me. I was left with nothing but scars.

BAILEY. You're all healed now.

RHONDA. My face, yes.

BAILEY. I understand.

RHONDA. Women do love money. And men have most of it.

BAILEY. Not this one. I do not have most of it.

RHONDA. What's a story worth, Bailey?

BAILEY. Not much, I guess.

RHONDA. And a man's only worth what he's got in the bank. Sorry. But she was right to leave you.

BAILEY. Yeah. The girl. But hard as she was, I wasn't killed for being worthless.

RHONDA. My husband fell. He got what he –

BAILEY. Deserved.

RHONDA. There was a time…when I first saw him…I dreamed of being in his arms. I wanted him more than anything in the world.

BAILEY. I know the feeling.

RHONDA. Then I got him. I'd like to be pleasantly surprised just once. By anything.

BAILEY. The night isn't over.

(RHONDA *looks away, on edge.*)

Not for us, anyway

(*another distant siren*)

For someone. But not for us.

(**BAILEY** *goes to the station door and opens it. He glances up and down the street, then steps back in.*)

BAILEY. *(cont.)* They'll work their way here for sure. Never had to figure a murder before. But they'll get here.

RHONDA. Maybe they've already caught him.

(*Another siren. They listen silently as it zooms by in the distance.* **BAILEY** *closes the door.*)

BAILEY. No. Somebody's on the run. With a whole bunch of money.

RHONDA. It's not safe anywhere, is it?

BAILEY. Even here. Even Thunder Bay. All it takes is the wrong kind getting in. One killing like this, and suddenly we're a vest-pocket metropolis. All because someone among us poisons the well with greed and violence.

RHONDA. Most people are killed by people they know. Even people they loved.

BAILEY. Like your husband.

RHONDA. Fair enough. And the man killed tonight, maybe another trapped wife.

BAILEY. She is trapped. But deep in the ground. He's a widower, Rhonda Claire. For many years now. See? Not all wives kill their husbands.

RHONDA. If you don't count dreams.

(*They go silent a moment;* **RHONDA** *particularly restless. She turns to the clock.*)

BAILEY. Clocks don't like to be looked at.

(**RHONDA** *turns away from the clock – and* **BAILEY**. **BAILEY** *studies her.*)

You have good posture. Usually the sign of a rigid upbringing.

(**RHONDA** *turns to him.*)

RHONDA. There's no end to you, is there.

BAILEY. *(laughs)* Well, eventually.

RHONDA. *(softly)* Not soon enough.

BAILEY. Wow.

RHONDA. *(flustered)* Sorry. It just slipped.

BAILEY. Like your husband.

(**RHONDA** *leaps up.*)

RHONDA. Stop saying that! People die! Accidents happen!!

BAILEY. Some accidents need help to happen.

RHONDA. Damn it, Bailey. I was fighting for my life. What would you have done??

BAILEY. I probably wouldn't have married for money in the first place.

RHONDA. It wasn't just that! And what business is it of yours!?

(She moves coldly to the counter, leaning, head in hand. **BAILEY** *rises slowly and moves to her.)*

BAILEY. *(gently)* Did you cry?

RHONDA. Cry? When he died?

BAILEY. At the funeral? When friends gathered?

RHONDA. Yes. Of course.

BAILEY. For show?

(**RHONDA** *turns to him.*)

RHONDA. *(softly)* Yes.

BAILEY. Things turned out well.

RHONDA. Everyone knew what I lived with.

BAILEY. But you cried for them.

RHONDA. I was his wife. Whatever the circumstances, it's expected.

BAILEY. Why can't a woman just say, 'He was an abusive bastard. I'm glad he's dead'? I mean, what would be the sin of a little gravesite candor?

(**RHONDA** *manages a small smile.*)

My view? Society needs a complete overhaul! Top to bottom! Inside out! Just gut it and start over!

(RHONDA laughs.)

BAILEY. *(cont.)* They should put a statue of you in Thunder Bay. The city is one bastard lighter thanks to you.

(RHONDA's smile vanishes.)

RHONDA. That's not funny, Bailey.

(BAILEY steps back from her.)

BAILEY. I'm just saying…what others might condemn in you…I admire.

(RHONDA looks at him.)

RHONDA. What are you getting at?

BAILEY. Just…the truth isn't always the most vital thing between people.

RHONDA. I've told you the truth.

BAILEY. Do you even know what the word means anymore, Rhonda Claire?

RHONDA. How dare you say that to me. Who are you to judge?

BAILEY. But that's just the point. I'm not judging you. Whatever the truth, whatever you've done, it's okay. A woman like you, you can't be expected to survive and prosper playing by the rules. And even…playing within the law. You're too, frankly, beautiful to pull through this life being ordinary. You can't go unnoticed anywhere. That makes it more difficult to get away with your crimes. What I'm saying, Rhonda Claire, is that they're not crimes if it's you at the top of the stairs, or getting high on the haze of a smoking gun. The law shouldn't apply to you, Rhonda Claire. The world still doesn't get women. If it did, you'd get that statue.

(RHONDA gazes at BAILEY a long moment.)

RHONDA. You think you know me? You think you know my life? My secrets? You call me a stranger, but pretend to read every inch of me. What gives, Bailey? You trying to psych me out? Bed me down? Have me tumble for a

fresh new crime because I got away with the first one?
What's going on in that story-teller head of yours?

BAILEY. I thought I was paying you a compliment.

RHONDA. By saying beauty excuses violence?

BAILEY. It's your out. What would you do without your
beauty?

RHONDA. You're making me something I'm not. I...I don't
kill people.

BAILEY. Except...

RHONDA. *(softly)* Yes. The man I once loved.

BAILEY. The man whose money you once loved.

RHONDA. I...never stopped loving his money. It just went
away.

BAILEY. Yeah. Money. When will it stop ruining lives?

RHONDA. I don't mind it. When I have it.

BAILEY. Well. Sure. But where do you get it?

(**RHONDA** *sighs and nods.*)

Got to get around. Got to always move. You don't get
it standing still.

RHONDA. It doesn't find you.

BAILEY. Sometimes it's just bumping into the right person.
Meeting someone new. Out of the blue. Like us. From
nowhere. This is how you grow. Being unstuck to
things.

RHONDA. People, too.

BAILEY. Well, if it's right–

RHONDA. It's never right, Bailey. People were never meant
to be together. I'm sure of it. It's always about getting
something. Cash. Or a body.

BAILEY. Either case, something to touch.

RHONDA. I'm tired of being something to touch, Bailey.

BAILEY. You don't mean never.

RHONDA. Maybe I do.

BAILEY. Unless there's a pay-off.

(**RHONDA** *flinches.*)

BAILEY. *(cont.)* I'm no fool anymore. I know a man's money outranks his flesh.

RHONDA. Don't go by me. I just came out this way.

BAILEY. It makes you think. What did he have planned for tomorrow?

RHONDA. Who?

BAILEY. The man tonight.

RHONDA. *(a whisper)* Oh.

BAILEY. I wonder if his last words…were the name of his killer. Like when your hus –

RHONDA. Stop that!

BAILEY. Don't you wish…you could take things back?

RHONDA. Reality has a nasty habit of being unavoidable.

BAILEY. That's why people like stories.

RHONDA. So why aren't you rich?

BAILEY. Not everybody likes the tales I tell. Occupational hazard, delving into the dark.

RHONDA. Well, you've got your next setting right here. God it's grim.

(**BAILEY** *looks around.*)

BAILEY. Yeah. This could be good. Something could happen here.

RHONDA. I'm glad this place inspires you.

BAILEY. That's why I say, I'm not for everybody.

RHONDA. Neither is bourbon, but it's still around. Though not close enough right now.

BAILEY. Be nice to have a bottle. We could drink to each other's health.

RHONDA. While secretly thinking the opposite.

(*They laugh.*)

BAILEY. You've got a streak in you.

RHONDA. It's just this night.

BAILEY. Yeah. Something just not quite right about it. And you...

RHONDA. Am I going to be your next story, Bailey?

BAILEY. You're like a character in one. In fact, you remind me of Marjorie Hollow. She was a character in one of my first stories. She had a bad marriage, too. So many good stories come from lousy marriages. She killed her husband, too. But it wasn't self-defense. She was having an affair with the kid that bagged her groceries. Barely a man when it started. Maybe seventeen. For Marjorie Hollow, it was all about kicks. When her husband balked, she riddled him with bullets. Just for being in the way.

RHONDA. What happened to her?

BAILEY. When the kid threatened to talk, she bagged him like he bagged her fruit. Emptied her pistol into his throat. Just to make the point.

RHONDA. Then what?

BAILEY. Marjorie Hollow got the chair. But that was just a kick, too. She shimmied on that fry-cooker like it was just some new dance. And it was. Her last dance.

RHONDA. You have any happy endings, Bailey?

BAILEY. Happy endings are for suckers. Even Old Yeller had to die.

RHONDA. I get out of here, it'll be a happy ending.

BAILEY. For who, Rhonda Claire?

RHONDA. For me. That okay?

BAILEY. No one is alone in their story.

RHONDA. I am. And that's the way it's going to stay.

BAILEY. You can't mean that.

RHONDA. What's it to you, anyway?

BAILEY. Nothing. Nothing.

(RHONDA *peers out a window, straining to look up the block.*)

RHONDA. *(muttering)* One time. Just one time...

(*She paces nervously.*)

BAILEY. At least it's quiet. The sirens have stopped.

(**RHONDA** *ignores him.*)

I guess he's at the morgue. One thing about a small town. Where-ever you live in it, you're near the morgue. That's at least some comfort. And our cemetery... I don't mean to brag, but it's beautiful. If they ever did make a postcard for this place, I'd say put the cemetery on it. It might just be our best thing.

RHONDA. *(muttering)* Heartwarming.

BAILEY. Even you might like it there.

RHONDA. I plan to die in Thunder Bay, if you don't mind.

BAILEY. Sure. I mean, that's where your husband's buried.

(**RHONDA** *bristles.*)

But if your plans change, and who knows what might happen between now and then, keep us in mind for your final resting place. They've got trees, a soft, rolling creek and one day they'll have me.

RHONDA. You have stock in that cemetery?

BAILEY. If only. It's packed. And just like that, here comes another customer. The only one with a bullet hole in him. He'll have lots to talk about. If, you know, you go on to some new place where you can talk. I think you do.

RHONDA. Maybe this is it. Maybe we got on that bus and died going over a cliff. Maybe this is where you wind up.

BAILEY. That would be disappointing. I pictured something more uplifting.

RHONDA. That's what makes us different. I know when the time comes it's going to be hot and it's going to be ugly. That's why it doesn't matter what you do on Earth. We all get what's coming when we close our eyes for the last time. Live in the moment and make it count. Words of wisdom from The Church Of Me.

BAILEY. You and church in the same breath?

RHONDA. What's that mean? I'm some kind of sinner because of the way I look? I'm a widow, Bailey. Have some compassion.

BAILEY. That was three years ago.

RHONDA. But I'm not remarried, am I?

BAILEY. I only know what you tell me.

RHONDA. You know I'm not. And never will be.

BAILEY. People say never. It doesn't mean anything. You meet a millionaire next week you'll forget you said never tonight. Unless…unless somehow…money's no longer a worry.

(RHONDA *is silent*)

Then…then maybe you could accept a man who isn't rich.

RHONDA. You think I'm one callous woman, don't you? Like the girl who left you. You see me, you see her. That right?

BAILEY. Pretty good for no degree.

RHONDA. What do you think you know about me, Bailey? You suspect me of killing that man tonight?

BAILEY. I'd be crazy not to. You hate men and you covet money. It adds up.

RHONDA. I don't hate men! I wish they were different, but I don't automatically hate them. I didn't hate you. At first.

BAILEY. We broke the thirty minute rule.

RHONDA. Anyway, hating men and wanting money aren't crimes.

BAILEY. No. But it fits tonight.

(RHONDA *takes a breath and looks hard at* BAILEY.)

RHONDA. You want me to be guilty,

(BAILEY *fidgets.*)

BAILEY. Maybe.

RHONDA. So you can turn me in and be a small town hero? Snatch up a husky reward?

BAILEY. We don't pay for good citizenship here. It's expected. And you might find this hard to believe...

(**BAILEY** *glumly turns away.*)

RHONDA. Yes?

(*He slowly turns to her.*)

BAILEY. I'm no hero, Rhonda Claire.

(*She looks at him a moment, a bit shaken.*)

RHONDA. Well...they're made up anyway.

BAILEY. Everyone in that cemetery...in every cemetery... could have used one in the end. And maybe you could use one now.

RHONDA. You think I'm that close, Bailey?.

BAILEY. You made your bed.

RHONDA. Who are you?

BAILEY. I'm not the stranger here.

RHONDA. I only know what you tell me.

BAILEY. It's just, I get a worried mind sometimes. Don't get me wrong. I want no harm to come to you. I know you're alone. And I know that's what you want. But with no one to turn to, particularly on this night... yeah, I fear you're that close.

(**RHONDA** *is suddenly anguished; agitated.*)

RHONDA. They have a restroom here?

(**BAILEY** *looks around*)

BAILEY. Over there.

(**RHONDA** *moves toward the rest-room, then grabs her bag.*)

I'm offended.

RHONDA. Good.

(*She goes into the restroom. The click of the door lock is audible.* **BAILEY** *paces pensively. He reaches into his bag and pulls out the voice recorder. He scans the depot, then speaks into the tiny machine.*)

BAILEY. His thoughts couldn't undo the knot of images in his head. The dead man bleeding into the carpet, and his killer, in her warped composure, primping in the mirror, adjusting her hair, applying a seductive drop of fragrance he knows, if he lives to reflect, he will never forget. There was still no moon, but in his mind, he pictured one. A big shimmery moon, illuminating her so mistily that only his fantasy of her emerged in the light. Her violence, the blood of her victims, her corrupted soul, obscured by the moon's limitations in one man's carefully sculpted illusion. He had only been in love once before, and figured this was probably not the most promising of circumstances to try again. Unless, he is wrong. But his sinking heart knows he's not. He knows he was born with the curse of never being wrong about people. And it is a curse, to be sure. No tailor-made moon, no winsome aroma, no nothing can change the hard facts. And he learned early in life that hard facts make up the world. Somewhere down the wet, murky highway, a bus is headed into town. It will pick up passengers destined for Thunder Bay. If there are any left standing when it gets here.

(**RHONDA** *steps out of the restroom as* **BAILEY** *quickly places his recorder back into his bag. He notes her alluring scent.*)

RHONDA. This town afford a scrub-brush?

BAILEY. I could have called the police while you were in there.

RHONDA. Why didn't you?

BAILEY. Maybe I have a soft spot for dangerous women. Marjorie Hollow smelled good, too. Desperate women are the best smelling women on the face of the earth. Marjorie Hollow did her hair like yours, too.

RHONDA. Marjorie Hollow isn't real. And she's dead.

BAILEY. Oh. Yeah.

RHONDA. You fancy yourself some dapper detective?

BAILEY. The suit? Off the rack.

RHONDA. You fill it out adequately. You'll land a girl some day.

BAILEY. I'd like that.

RHONDA. Maybe one who hasn't fallen from grace.

BAILEY. I could catch her before she hits the ground.

RHONDA. Or at least one who doesn't have you looking over your shoulder all the time wondering if she's going to kill you.

BAILEY. It's always going to be something.

(They exchange a small smile.)

Is this your round about way of confessing? Or...testing my tolerance for a future with you?

*(**RHONDA**'s smile widens.)*

RHONDA. Is this your round about way of confessing you're after me? And not just for supposedly snuffing out the town tycoon?

BAILEY. You put on fresh perfume in the restroom. For the bus driver?

RHONDA. Oh, Bailey. It's just habit. Don't you know women at all?

BAILEY. Sure. You want to look nice. Smell nice. I get it. But in a dive like this?

RHONDA. You see yourself in the mirror...sometimes you forget where you are for a second.

BAILEY. If you're dazzled by your reflection.

RHONDA. Okay. I'm not disappointed in my face.

BAILEY. Or anything south of it.

RHONDA. So hang me.

BAILEY. Don't joke. If they catch you –

RHONDA. They'll be wasting their time.

BAILEY. You mean...if you get across the border first.

RHONDA. I mean I didn't shoot him. I don't even like guns.

BAILEY. You don't have to like a gun to use a gun. And you don't have to like a town to feel the compulsion to visit it. What pulled you here, Rhonda Claire? What enticed you to come from so far away to this barely noticeable place?

RHONDA. That's personal.

BAILEY. Sex?

RHONDA. There's plenty of sex in Thunder Bay.

BAILEY. Maybe. But there's all kinds of sex. And maybe the kind you wanted, the kind you desperately needed, wasn't there. Maybe it was here, of all places. Here in the little town…where I was born.

RHONDA. *(unnerved)* What do you know about sex, anyway? When was the last time you held a girl?

BAILEY. I'm holding one right now.

RHONDA. I'm trapped here by a slow bus. Not you!

BAILEY. Trapped. Always trapped.

RHONDA. Yes, Bailey. But I always pry loose.

BAILEY. Some day, something unforeseen could keep you trapped forever.

RHONDA. Like you?

BAILEY. Well, you have to admit…I'm unforeseen.

RHONDA. Why do you want to trap me, Bailey? What do you think you have in me? Am I your ticket to euphoria? Go trap something of value. Something that has meaning. Something that can't…that can't hurt you.

(**RHONDA** *is clearly upset.* **BAILEY** *takes a breath.*)

BAILEY. *(gently)* The bus isn't slow. We're just early.

(silence)

You should have just stayed where you were a little longer.

(**RHONDA** *ignores him.*)

It had to be better than here.

(silence)

Or was it?

(**RHONDA** *is tight-lipped, feeling…well, trapped.*)

BAILEY. *(cont.)* What could be worse than this God-forsaken tinderbox? Yeah. You should have stayed put. Killed time where you were. Unless…

(**RHONDA** *looks at him grimly.*)

You had to get out of there. Just like you have to get of here. Maybe…maybe something happened that wasn't supposed to happen.

RHONDA. *(softly)* Don't.

BAILEY. All of a sudden. An unexpected thing. Life throws you a curve at a hundred and fifty miles an hour. You don't move fast, you're knocked out cold. I could tell. You walked in here winded and tangled up tight. You got here fast all right. From where? What happened tonight, Rhonda Claire?

RHONDA. *(distraught)* It's…personal.

BAILEY. I won't tell.

RHONDA. There's nothing to tell! There's nothing there.

BAILEY. Yes there is, Rhonda Claire. There's something –

RHONDA. No. No.

BAILEY. On the floor.

(**RHONDA** *is jolted.*)

RHONDA. You're…you're imagining me, Bailey. You're a storyteller. You make things up. That's what storytellers do. Right?

BAILEY. Right.

RHONDA. You're pretending things about me. To pass the time. To create a new story to tell in Thunder Bay. You're turning me into something, into merchandise, to have something to sell. Right?

BAILEY. *(softly)* Wrong. I don't want to sell you, Rhonda Claire. I want to save you.

RHONDA. Save yourself, Bailey.

BAILEY. I know. Men in your orbit don't last long.

RHONDA. That's a lie. Like everything else. I'm better to men than they are to me. I've been smacked, slugged, stripped, shammed, shamed, smothered, shocked and stung in every way conceivable. I shouldn't even be alive. How many women are not? At the hands of men who loved them. Who wrote poetry to them. Who... saved them.

BAILEY. All men could die as far as I'm concerned. I'd probably do a lot better with women if I were the only man on Earth.

RHONDA. Don't bet on it.

BAILEY. *(laughing)* Yeah. You're right. You've either got it or you don't.

RHONDA. I was just...being mean.

BAILEY. I got you hot, didn't I? I mean, under the collar.

RHONDA. My heart's still racing. I mean, because you got me so angry.

BAILEY. Am I imagining you as something you're not?

RHONDA. You killed off Marjorie Hollow. Maybe that was a mistake.

BAILEY. Oh, no. She had to pay for what she did. People need closure.

RHONDA. *(delicately)* People? Or you?

(**BAILEY** *looks down, shuffling a bit.*)

Bailey Bryce. What have you done?

BAILEY. Nothing.

RHONDA. Then what's been done to you?

BAILEY. *(softly)* Somebody.

RHONDA. Somebody what?

BAILEY. Somebody took...what was mine.

RHONDA. Who? What did they take?

BAILEY. The only thing that matters, Rhonda Claire.

RHONDA. Money?

BAILEY. That's right.

RHONDA. When?

BAILEY. Tonight.

RHONDA. Tonight?? What kind of pit of a town is this?

BAILEY. It seemed so normal. So safe. Until...

RHONDA. Until I got here?

(**BAILEY** *and* **RHONDA** *stare each other down.* **RHONDA** *lifts her travel bag and slams it down on the bench.*)

(*fuming*) You think this bag is crammed with money?

BAILEY. You tell me.

RHONDA. How do I know *you're* not the killer?

(**BAILEY** *freezes for a moment.*)

BAILEY. I'm from here.

RHONDA. Yeah. You are. And you know everything about everybody. Including who's rich and who's not. How do I know *your* bag isn't filled with blood-soaked bills?

BAILEY. Interesting.

RHONDA. You have a thing for me, don't you?

BAILEY. That's right.

RHONDA. Don't pursue me in Thunder Bay. I told you. I'm through with love.

BAILEY. But not with sex. The kind of sex that pays off big. Where will you go next, Rhonda Claire? Or can you retire on tonight's haul?

(**RHONDA** *sits tensely, clutching her travel bag. She looks nervously at her watch, keeping her gaze away from* **BAILEY**. *She strains to appear composed.* **BAILEY** *does not take his eyes off her.*)

The way you're sitting there. It's a trick. You're not looking at me. But I'm all you see in your mind. You're wondering what to do with me. There's no one here, you're thinking. You can take the pistol from your bag, shoot me dead, and drag my body off somewhere before the bus arrives to take you home. Who will ever know, you're thinking. This guy follows me to Thunder Bay, I'll never know a moment's peace, you're thinking. I can kill him there, on my own turf, you're thinking, but that's risky, with a dead husband on my record, you're thinking. Remarkable how serene you appear,

Rhonda Claire, with such grave thoughts clouding your head. You could step outside for some air and then disappear. You've got plenty of cash. You could fly to Thunder Bay and go in style. But they do check those bags, don't they? Sure. The bus is slower, but safer, isn't it? No one expects a wealthy woman to take a bus. Yeah. You can lose this town, Rhonda Claire. But you'll never lose me. Even if you killed me right now, I'm all you'd see in Thunder Bay. On every street. In every alley. In every dream. You're no Marjorie Hollow. She smelled like lilies, but had no conscience. You do, Rhonda Claire. And that's your fatal flaw. I tell stories. There's truth in every one of them. I can tell by the way you're sitting there, ignoring me desperately, that I've captured the essence of your truth. The essence of truth isn't evidence, sure. But it's close enough for me. I'm not your judge, Rhonda Claire. I'm not your moral guide. I'm just a well dressed weaver of tales, waiting for a bus, or something even greater, who knows your scent, your destination, and your secrets.

(There is a tense silence. Suddenly, **RHONDA** *grabs* **BAILEY** *'s bag and opens it. She reaches in and pulls out a handful of blood-stained money.* **BAILEY** *is jolted.)*

RHONDA. *(frenzied)* What's *your* secret, Bailey Bryce??

*(***BAILEY** *is shaken, riveted.)*

You're a weaver of tales, all right!

(She pulls more wads of cash out of **BAILEY** *'s bag.)*

It's the stolen money! And the dead man's blood! In your bag!

BAILEY. *(rattled)* No. It's mine.

RHONDA. I'm the one who should call the police.

BAILEY. What...what tipped you off?

RHONDA. Money has an aroma all its own.

BAILEY. So does blood.

RHONDA. You said you were robbed tonight.

BAILEY. I was.

RHONDA. This bag is stuffed–

BAILEY. It's a lot. But not all of it.

RHONDA. *(cautiously)* What happened tonight, Bailey?

(**BAILEY** *looks at her deeply.*)

BAILEY. I killed him.

(**RHONDA** *buckles. She sits tensely.*)

RHONDA. For the money?

BAILEY. Why else?

(**RHONDA**'s *breaths come fast. She fights to compose herself.*)

RHONDA. Where's the rest of it?

BAILEY. I don't have it.

RHONDA. You were robbed. Coming here?

BAILEY. Don't be afraid.

(she turns to him)

RHONDA. I'm not.

BAILEY. You're less than five feet away from me.

RHONDA. But…but your bag is closer to me than you.

(tense silence)

Is the gun still in it?

BAILEY. You can find out.

RHONDA. You want my prints on it.

BAILEY. *(smiles)* Yeah. You've been around the block.

RHONDA. *(breathless)* Have *you*, Bailey? Have *you* been around the block?

BAILEY. I've never been anywhere. I want tonight to change my life.

RHONDA. By confessing to a murder?

BAILEY. It's a start.

(**RHONDA** *slowly rises.*)

RHONDA. Why are you confiding in me?

BAILEY. Why lie now? You see the money. You have the proof. What should I say? I don't know how it got there?

*(**RHONDA** is baffled, unsure)*

RHONDA. So, you're not going to Thunder Bay to peddle stories. You're going there to hide.

BAILEY. Oh, I'll tell stories there. But, yeah, I'll be hiding, too. Maybe you know places to disappear.

RHONDA. *(on edge)* Why Thunder Bay?

BAILEY. It's where the last bus goes.

RHONDA. You put a lot of faith in a stranger.

BAILEY. You're the only stranger I know. And killers have no friends.

RHONDA. Why shouldn't I talk?

BAILEY. We're kindred spirits.

RHONDA. Oh, Bailey –

BAILEY. You can turn me in.

(He steps closer to her.)

Or you can turn me loose.

RHONDA. You don't need me to get away. You just need a bus.

BAILEY. I want to escape from here. But not...from you.

*(**RHONDA** looks at him; tense, torn.)*

I have money.

RHONDA. There's blood on it.

BAILEY. Nothing devalues cash. Even the most delicate slim smooth hand will gladly take it unclean.

RHONDA. You don't respect me, do you?

BAILEY. My God. More than anything.

*(**RHONDA**, speechless, gazes at him. She catches herself and turns away. She is thrown; disquieted.)*

Penny for your thoughts.

*(**RHONDA**, fraught, avoids his gaze.)*

How 'bout a hundred grand?

RHONDA. *(anxious)* Stop trying to buy me.

BAILEY. All right. Forget that part of it. This is why I hate money. This is why there's got to be something else. Something else that matters to you.

RHONDA. *(bitterly)* Like what, Bailey? What would that be? What else can a man give me anymore?

(beat)

BAILEY. Devotion.

RHONDA. *(struck)* Devotion?

BAILEY. It's a kind of currency if that helps.

RHONDA. What are you driving at?

BAILEY. In your whole life, Rhonda Claire, through all you've experienced and endured. All the passion and loss. Have you ever–ever–met a man…like me?

(RHONDA looks at him apprehensively.)

A man this profoundly devoted to you.

(RHONDA buckles. She sits tensely.)

Think back. Be fair. Just for a moment. Just for me. Has any man been willing to do for you what I have done in a small town minute? Has any man you've ever known – ever loved - gone this far for you? Right up to the brink…and over it?

RHONDA. I don't understand –

BAILEY. Come on. Come on.

(RHONDA is quaking. She struggles to settle herself.)

RHONDA. Are you ready…ready to confess to the killing?

BAILEY. Let's go.

RHONDA. *(staggered)* Why?? What are you trying to prove??

(He moves close to her.)

BAILEY. That something besides money can have worth. That a man can give you something of great import that doesn't fit into a purse.

RHONDA. What does your confession give to me?

BAILEY. Your life, of course.

RHONDA. You make no sense.

(He moves closer to her.)

BAILEY. I saw you.

RHONDA. Saw me what?

BAILEY. Gun him down. I saw him convulsing on the floor. And die.

RHONDA. *(startled)* You saw no such thing!

BAILEY. I was there. I watched it unfold before my eyes, like a story come to life. The woman from Thunder Bay, pulling the gun, pulling the trigger and pulling the heist. That you did the killing was almost too incredible. I planned it so carefully myself. I thought God is smiling on me tonight. But when you went for the money, I thought maybe there is no God. It wasn't an impulsive crime of passion, I realized. It was a robbery. I panicked, though what you dropped and left behind could fill a man's bank account nicely.

*(***BAILEY*** suddenly grabs ***RHONDA****'s bag and opens it, yanking out wads and wads of money.)*

However, what you got away with could bring a man, and a woman, luxury for a long, long time.

*(***RHONDA*** is jolted.)*

I thought it would all be mine. So I could finally have what I wanted. Just this one time in my life…when I would finally get…

RHONDA. What, Bailey? The girl?

BAILEY. *(softly)* Yeah. I've watched you for days. With him. He bragged about a beautiful Canadian he met on a trip there, who was traveling here to visit him. Talked about marrying you.

RHONDA. He said that?

BAILEY. He loved you, Rhonda Claire.

RHONDA. It wasn't mutual.

BAILEY. You acted like it was. You were all hands.

RHONDA. That's not love, Bailey.

BAILEY. I know that. You know that. But he wanted to believe what he wanted to believe.

RHONDA. Like you. Wanting to believe if you had all his money, I'd go right into your lap.

BAILEY. I thought he was dumb. But he and I aren't so far apart, are we?

RHONDA. Well, he's dead.

BAILEY. Love is a killer. I wanted you so much, so fast... I mean, I was all prepared to shoot that filthy rich pigeon –

RHONDA. I saved you a bullet.

BAILEY. You got that right.

RHONDA. Sure. Now I get the picture. You thought taking the fall for me –

BAILEY. Might make you...well, fall for me. I was flailing.

RHONDA. That's devotion, all right. Kill for me. Lie for me. There's almost nothing left.

BAILEY. You're so stunningly ice cold, I should have worn a hat.

RHONDA. I urged you to avoid me.

BAILEY. It was too late. I'd been watching you too long. And no man watching you could avoid falling in love with you.

RHONDA. Even as I shot one dead?

BAILEY. There's plenty of others. Like the one right here. The one who could turn you in if his bitterness pushed him that way.

RHONDA. You'd do that to me?

BAILEY. Why not? You've ruined this town. And you've ruined me.

RHONDA. You're not ruined, Bailey. Just a little damaged. And I know damage when I see it because I've had to repair my own over and over again. That's life, Bailey. You get a little damaged every day. That's, after all, why women wear make-up. Men have to cling to being stoic. Tough faces are their make-up. Toughen up that face, Bailey. You'll never get a woman like me looking so...female.

BAILEY. You're so sure I won't call the police, aren't you? You shouldn't be. This is my last power grab.

RHONDA. For what? My undying love?

BAILEY. *(snapping)* WHAT IN GOD'S NAME IS WRONG WITH LOVE??

(**RHONDA**, *a bit startled, looks at* **BAILEY** *a long moment.*)

RHONDA. It makes people yell.

(**BAILEY** *breathes heavily; winded, distraught*)

It makes people sad and bewildered, off their game and dangerously distracted. You came this close to killing for it. And for what? *(indicating herself)* For this. For silken-skinned, sweet-smelling immorality.

BAILEY. Yeah. You've turned me into some-thing.

RHONDA. For tonight. You can turn back tomorrow. When I'm far away from you.

(**BAILEY** *looks at her hard.*)

BAILEY. Maybe...I can't turn back. I stole money and schemed to end a life for my own gratification. And it didn't bother me a bit, when I thought of what it was going to get me. And even now, I wish I could flip back time and get to him before you did. Even now, I wish I had killed and robbed for you. Because I'm still so sure...had I really done it...you'd be swept off your God-damned feet and into my dire arms.

(**RHONDA** *is quiet a moment.*)

RHONDA. You might have something there.

(**BAILEY** *looks at her, surprised.*)

But we can't have a 'do over' here, can we? He's already dead and I have the bulk of the money.

(**BAILEY** *is crestfallen, but not finished.*)

BAILEY. You're forgetting. I'm a witness. I've still got the power to take it all away.

RHONDA. Leaving you with what?

BAILEY. It would keep you here. Close to me.

RHONDA. You want to watch me rot in prison?

(**BAILEY** *is torn.*)

Why don't you remember me as I am right now? Healthy, wealthy and a little bit happy. And if you want, you can write a story about me. Even this one. Just change my name, if you don't mind. See? You get something, too. Not to mention enough money to satisfy yourself, and maybe the next girl who struts into this strange stretch of nowhere looking to transform her life. Just make sure she's not too much like me. Especially the gun part.

BAILEY. *(lost)* No one's like you, Rhonda Claire.

RHONDA. And that's a good thing.

(**RHONDA** *glances to the clock. It's getting closer to 2 am.*)

RHONDA. I hated that clock when I first got here. Now, not so much.

BAILEY. Even from the window…there was something about you. Like Marjorie Hollow herself stepped out of a dream, and into my life. Scent and all. The hair. The moves. The ease that accompanies the violence. Everything. Everything but the joy Marjorie Hollow experienced ending lives. I could see on your face when you pulled the trigger…there was no joy. I'm kind of glad. It's a redeeming thing, not to enjoy it.

RHONDA. I didn't want to kill him, but he was onto me. You see my fix, don't you?

BAILEY. He was no small kill. He's well connected in this town. He could have made life Hell for you.

RHONDA. So it was justified.

BAILEY. I'm sold. But I'm not the law.

RHONDA. You won't do me in, will you?

BAILEY. You go down, I go down.

RHONDA. Yeah. We're both in this.

BAILEY. And we're both going to Thunder Bay.

(**RHONDA**'s *mind is racing*)

RHONDA. Maybe we shouldn't be in the same place, Bailey.

BAILEY. Come on. Thunder Bay's big enough for both of us.

RHONDA. I don't like it. We were both in that house. Two people leaving this little town on the same night. Both going to Canada? It looks bad.

(**BAILEY** *sizes her up.*)

BAILEY. Sure. I get it. Look, I won't crowd you, Rhonda Claire. I've got a life of my own.

RHONDA. You said it yourself. You'll be everywhere.

(**BAILEY** *studies her as she seals up her bag.*)

BAILEY. Someone waiting?

RHONDA. What?

BAILEY. Back home. You've got somebody?

RHONDA. I've got no one. I told you. That's the way it is. That's the way I want it. And that's the way it's going to be. You don't need me, Bailey. Any woman you'd pick off the street at random would be better than me. And you deserve better than me. A woman could do worse than Bailey Bryce.

BAILEY. Not after tonight. Not after all this.

(**BAILEY** *looks at the clock.*)

Maybe I can start over again –

RHONDA. In Thunder Bay?

BAILEY. I can't hide out in town.

RHONDA. Sure you can. They know you here. They'd never suspect you of anything. I mean, look at you. And anyway, you're, at worst, guilty of finding some money.

You can say you heard the gunshot, ran into the house to help, and snatched up the cash so the killer couldn't grab more for himself. And if you can say *him*self, I'd consider it a personal favor.

BAILEY. But then I have to give it back. I don't want to give it back.

RHONDA. I thought you hated money.

BAILEY. It's tricky. I only wanted it to give to you so you would in turn give something to me.

RHONDA. My heart.

BAILEY. That was the theory.

RHONDA. My heart stays right where it is.

BAILEY. It's not a literal transaction.

RHONDA. Let's not get our hearts mangled up in this. You're Lover's Lane. I'm Lover's Leap. We're no couple.

(**BAILEY** *looks at her with a small smile.*)

BAILEY. I did get to you a little bit, didn't I?

(**RHONDA***'s about to protest, but yields.*)

RHONDA. Okay, Bailey. Yeah. A little bit.

BAILEY. I think you want me on that bus with you.

RHONDA. *(snapping)* I don't!

BAILEY. You'll miss me someday. When that cash dries up. And you're the kind of woman who likes to spend.

RHONDA. And where will your stash be? Under the mattress??

BAILEY. Maybe you'll find out someday.

RHONDA. Get off this, Bailey.

BAILEY. You'll miss me. I swear you will.

RHONDA. I won't! This heart beats only for me!

BAILEY. You're going to be a lonely woman, Rhonda Claire.

RHONDA. *(a clutch in her throat)* I know I will! So what? In the end, they only make caskets for one. I'll be used to it by then.

(**BAILEY** *sits.*)

BAILEY. I'll miss your chill on hot summer nights.

RHONDA. You won't even remember this down the road.

BAILEY. The night I fell in love with a woman who shot a man in cold blood? I think I'll remember. You?

RHONDA. I'm on that bus, you and what's his name are a distant memory.

BAILEY. What's his name? You mean, the dead guy?

RHONDA. What dead guy?

(**BAILEY** *gives her a look. She laughs.*)

See? I'm that good at forgetting.

(**BAILEY** *is amused – for a second.*)

BAILEY. This'll eat at you.

RHONDA. He's just a blur to me.

BAILEY. He is. But I'm not. I don't think you'll shake me so fast.

RHONDA. The girl who left you years ago, she shook you quick enough.

BAILEY. You've got a mouth like a knife.

RHONDA. Still want me?

BAILEY. This is where I first saw you. Right here. The day you got off the bus. I had to see what all the talk was about. In the days I shadowed you, I envisioned us together forever. Running away to some pretty place, set for life, everything we dreamed. Even making it legal and having a kid –

RHONDA. Have you lost your mind? You and me making a kid? Haven't we done enough??

BAILEY. It'd be part me. I'm not so bad.

RHONDA. The hell you're not, Mr. Bus Stop stalker. You think you're clean because you didn't pull that trigger yourself? You've got a killer's soul and you know it. One day you'll do it for sure. Why, you'd do it for me in a second, wouldn't you?

(**BAILEY** *is torn.*)

Wouldn't you?

BAILEY. *(softly)* Yes.

RHONDA. You don't become what you are in a couple of days. It's always there, Bailey. It was always in you, I'm sorry to say. I might have brought it out this time, but something will again. Maybe…maybe something did before. I don't know your past. I'd like to track down that girl and buy her a drink. Find out who you really are.

BAILEY. Don't waste your time.

RHONDA. Why? What'cha do to her?

BAILEY. I just mean…I don't deny it. I always knew I was no good. I just never knew how far I'd go. Yeah. I've done things. I can't look at the people here anymore. I've gone way over the line, Rhonda Claire.

RHONDA. Fine. Then get out. But not with me. We've got to remain far apart and forget this night ever happened. You've got to let go, Bailey. Of me. Of the dead man. Of your delusions. Cling only to the money, Bailey. Cling only to the money.

*(**BAILEY** steps closer to her.)*

BAILEY. I don't back down…If I insist on going with you, will you pull that gun from your bag and shoot me dead?

RHONDA. Let's not find out.

*(**RHONDA** looks to the clock.)*

BAILEY. Not much time. Once that bus gets here, you've got witnesses.

RHONDA. No one believes bus people.

BAILEY. Nevertheless.

RHONDA. Don't press me, Bailey. You know what I'm capable of. I just want to leave quietly, like I was never here in the first place.

BAILEY. If it were only so.

RHONDA. Knock off the sorrow. I woke you up. You needed this. Sometimes a kick is just the thing. What were you before I got here? Huh?

(**BAILEY** *sits by his travel bag.*)

BAILEY. Yeah. You couldn't tell me from anybody else. I'm not anybody else anymore.

RHONDA. You're carrying a dead man's money and a loaded gun. You're not like them, Bailey Bryce. You're like me. We're in a club now. And the one rule of survival in this club is that we don't endanger each other being fools.

(**BAILEY**'s *hand moves along his bag.*)

I know what you're thinking. Pull that gun, take me down, and have all the money for yourself. I'd have no regard for you at all if it didn't cross your mind.

BAILEY. Well...more of a flash than a cross –

RHONDA. Me, too. As soon as you started asking questions, probing me like a hot stick, I thought just shoot him. They can only execute you once.

BAILEY. Jeez. The make-pretend mother of our make-pretend child.

RHONDA. Lord knows I had plenty of time to bury you somewhere before the stage clip-clopped in.

BAILEY. Why didn't you?

RHONDA. I don't know what held me back. Curiosity. A little bit of fear. The fact that, and don't take this the wrong way, you're kind of...gentle.

(**BAILEY** *is thrown; a bit embarrassed.*)

That's how I know you won't go for that gun. And that's why I won't go for mine. Unless...unless you give me no choice. I'll admit it, and don't read into this, but I think it would haunt me if I killed you. The others, a pang maybe, but you...you'd bother me a long time.

BAILEY. I'll take that as a compliment.

(**RHONDA** *sits next to* **BAILEY**. *Not close, but not that far. She moves her bag next to her, very close. They sit quietly, both fidgety, glancing at the clock, which nears 2 am.*)

RHONDA. I'll be glad to wash this town off me.

BAILEY. You did all right here, I'd say.

(RHONDA *moves away from him.* BAILEY *stands, but keeps his distance.*)

Don't get on that bus. Stay with me tonight. Before the sun comes up, we'll be on our way where no one knows anybody or anything about anything. My money is your money. There's nothing you can want that you won't get.

(*She turns to him.*)

RHONDA. (*softly*) Except home.

BAILEY. People like us…can't be home anymore.

RHONDA. And people like us can never be attached to each other. Trust me, Bailey. I've been despicable longer than you. I know what works and what doesn't. You want something normal out of this. You're not seeing straight. We've got to make this night go away, and that has no chance of happening unless we never see each other again.

BAILEY. I've waited here a long time to let that bus leave without me on it.

(BAILEY *looks to the window, then back to the clock.*)

I've got to fall out of love with you in less than ten minutes.

RHONDA. Bailey.

BAILEY. Tell me how.

RHONDA. I snore.

(BAILEY *manages a smile.*)

How about this? I'm a bad kisser.

BAILEY. That'll be the day.

RHONDA. Really. I'm all surface. Take away the cut of my jib, you've got nothing you'd want to chase.

(BAILEY *looks at her a long moment.*)

BAILEY. Kiss me, Rhonda Claire.

RHONDA. Bailey. That simply is not going to happen.

BAILEY. Jesus. A kiss?

RHONDA. We'd have to get close to kiss. It's a mistake, Bailey.

BAILEY. You kissed the dead man plenty.

RHONDA. Not *when* he was dead. Please. Let's keep the story straight.

BAILEY. Would you kiss me for all the cash in my bag?

RHONDA. That's an unkind question. Look, don't make the situation more harrowing than it already is. Let's make our last few minutes here a bit more bubbly.

BAILEY. You can turn on a dime, can't you. Even in high-heels.

RHONDA. I'd have died at the bottom of a flight of stairs if I couldn't.

BAILEY. Yeah. People underestimate footwork.

(**BAILEY** *reaches out his hand.*)

Let's see what you've got.

(**RHONDA** *looks at him quizzically.*)

Dance with me, Rhonda Claire.

(**RHONDA** *shakes her head.*)

RHONDA. Get help, Bailey.

BAILEY. Try me. Maybe I'm good.

RHONDA. I'd say there's no music, but I'm afraid you'd start singing.

BAILEY. I'm just trying to keep things light, like you said. Make our last moments together pleasant.

RHONDA. This is about touching me.

BAILEY. So what?

RHONDA. You know my policy.

BAILEY. Maybe *you* should get help.

RHONDA. I help myself, Bailey.

(**BAILEY** *lowers his arm*)

BAILEY. You're not easy. At least with your clothes on.

(**RHONDA** *turns on him*)

RHONDA. Take that back!!

BAILEY. *(the clock)* It took less than a minute to kill your husband. It took less than a minute to kill the rich man tonight. It would take less than a minute to kill me now.

RHONDA. What are you – ??

BAILEY. *(hears something)* Shush.

(*He goes to the window, his back to* **RHONDA**.)

Yeah. I think I see headlights in the distance. It won't be long now...

(**RHONDA** *quietly reaches into her bag –*)

BAILEY. Yeah. I think that's it.

(**BAILEY** *turns just as* **RHONDA** *pulls her hand from the bag. She's clutching a large wad of cash. She holds it out to him.*)

BAILEY. What's that for?

RHONDA. Take it. It's a Thank You.

BAILEY. For what?

RHONDA. For not hurting me. For not killing me, despite my occasional cruelty. For offering to take the fall. For offering to die for me. For offering me the chance to kill you before the bus pulls in. I know you want me, but this money is like a piece of me. Maybe the best part of me. And I want to thank you most of all...

BAILEY. For what?

RHONDA. For not getting on the bus to Thunder Bay.

(**BAILEY** *looks to the window.*)

BAILEY. I'm still torn.

RHONDA. Let's make it a clean break. Let's give this story a happy ending.

BAILEY. Not for me.

RHONDA. Then for me. I could use one.

(The bus is heard approaching deep in the distance. RHONDA and BAILEY turn to the window. RHONDA extends her money-filled hand desperately to BAILEY.)

Please. Take it. Take it.

(BAILEY looks to the window, then to her, glumly.)

BAILEY. You don't have to bribe me, Rhonda Claire. Take my farewell as a parting gift.

RHONDA. You sure? I won't cry. Much.

BAILEY. You earned that money. Sort of. Put it away.

(RHONDA puts the money back snugly in her travel bag and zips it up.)

RHONDA. What are you going to do without me, Bailey?

BAILEY. Try to make sense of it.

RHONDA. It?

BAILEY. Life.

RHONDA. I hope…I hope you meet somebody who can love you back.

BAILEY. I gave it all I had tonight. If I only had it in me to just –

(The bus horn is heard, closing in. BAILEY swallows hard. RHONDA turns to the clock.)

RHONDA. Early. See, Bailey? Anything can happen.

(RHONDA, barely containing her excitement and glee, takes her bag and moves toward the door.)

BAILEY. *(downhearted)* Need a hand?

RHONDA. Lugging money is pure pleasure. And, amazingly, with all I've got in here, it still weighs less than a man.

(the sound and headlights of the bus rolling in.)

RHONDA. *(in awe)* It's here. It's actually here!

(BAILEY and RHONDA look at each other a long moment. BAILEY is clearly wrought and dejected.)

You can get the door.

(**BAILEY** *snaps out of it and holds the door open for her. The bus awaits outside the depot, engine idling.* **RHONDA** *begins to leave and turns to* **BAILEY**.)

RHONDA. *(cont.)* If you're ever in Thunder Bay... Oops. Habit.

BAILEY. Get there safely, Rhonda Claire.

RHONDA. Sorry to be smiling when I'm saying good-bye.

(She moves to leave. **BAILEY** *braces himself.)*

BAILEY. One thing before you go.

(**BAILEY** *suddenly and forcefully takes* **RHONDA** *into his arms and kisses her long and hard.* **RHONDA**'*s bag drops as the depot door closes. She breaks out of his grip, flustered and rattled.)*

RHONDA. *(shaken, mussed)* Bailey! How dare you.

(**BAILEY**'*s a bit dazed by his own sudden move.* **RHONDA** *hurriedly, angrily collects herself, straightens her hair and tousled skirt, then, a bit wobbled, grabs her bag.)*

(**BAILEY** *opens the door for her again.* **RHONDA** *looks at him, seething.)*

Women don't like that!

(She storms out. **BAILEY** *watches as she boards the bus. In a moment, the bus is heard pulling away into the night.* **BAILEY** *stares out as the sight and sound of the bus fade. He steps back, letting the depot door close.* **BAILEY** *scans the deserted station and sighs deeply. He goes to his bag and sits pensively. He reaches into his bag, through all the stained money, and pulls out his voice recorder, switching it on.)*

BAILEY. The night grew darker, but he was convinced the memory of her would never fade. He was convinced, too, that there was no mercy for sinners, despite the rumor that anybody seeking salvation can be saved. That was just more bunk in a world teetering under the sheer weight of it all. A world of swindlers, liars and killers, much like himself. He always knew he was one of them, one of the damned he knew so well because he knew himself best of all. And when he met her, that woman from Thunder Bay, he thought those sins might just fetch him a tidy prize. Something to hold dear besides money and sharp suits. But the woman from Thunder Bay had it right. Deadly people shouldn't mate. They should leave the world nothing to remember them by. They should just go quietly. Like they were never there. Like the moon, which hasn't been out for as long as he can remember.

(He takes a world-weary breath.)

Of course, he can only remember the night she left him. It will play over and over again in his mind. He can always toss in the moon for atmosphere. But once you open up that Pandora's Box, tampering with harsh reality, it could lead to anything. Like instead of her going all the way home, she gets off the bus a block away, and comes back to him.

(RHONDA *suddenly, silently, appears in the doorway.* **BAILEY,** *his back to her, continues speaking into the recorder.)*

His weary, jaded eyes became starry eyes. He didn't like it. Not one bit. Next, there'd be tears. The woman was right again. A man must have a tough face to get through life. He put his on, hoping it didn't look fake, which it was, wondering if a woman will ever kiss it again.

(He clicks off the recorder and the stage bumps to black.)

THE END

PROPERTIES PLOT

All props are carried onto the stage by the actors.

BAILEY BRYCE
Travel bag (on entrance)
Blood-stained cash (in bag)
Pocket size voice recorder (in bag)

RHONDA CLAIRE
Red Travel bag (on entrance)
Blood-stained cash (in bag)
Compact/accessories (in bag - optional)

COSTUME PLOT

There are no costume changes.

BAILEY BRYCE
A suit. Not overly flashy, but definitely small-town impressive.

RHONDA CLAIRE
Anything that sizzles. Sexy; high-end. Perhaps a pencil skirt, blouse and high heels. Bold, but classy. Fitted jacket optional. No glaring jewelry.

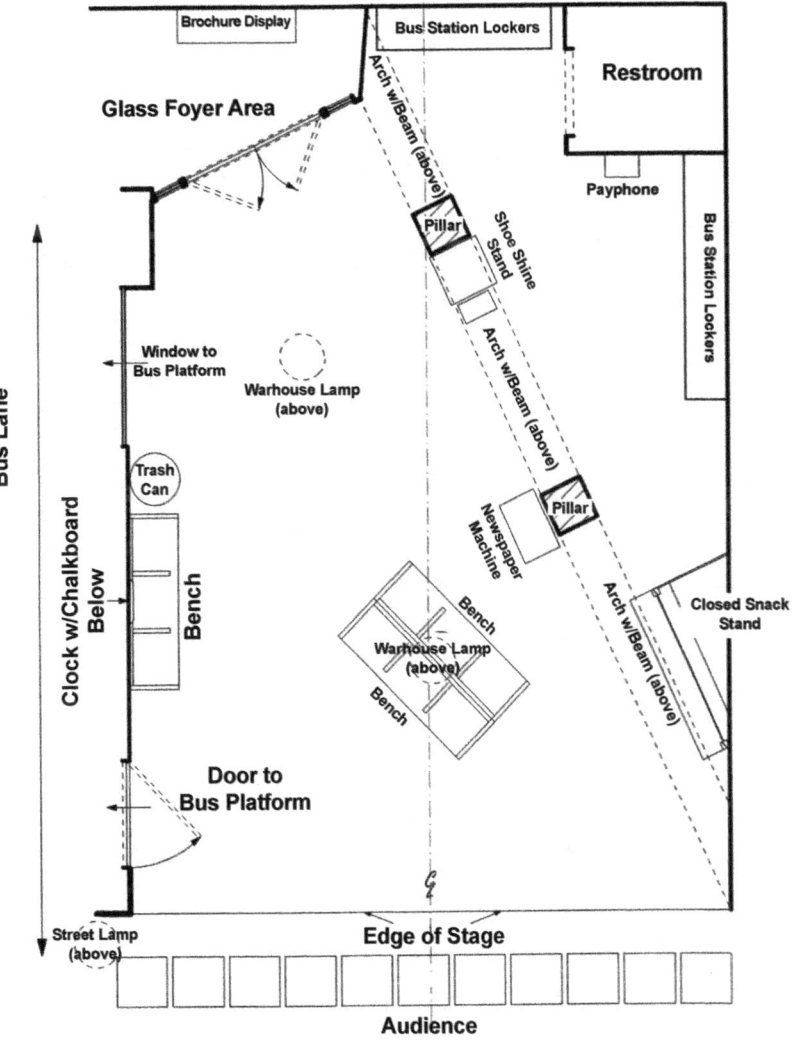

Set Design by Jessica Parks